First Little Readers™

The Queen's New Cat

by Liza Charlesworth

ISBN: 978-1-338-29794-2

Illustrated by Tammie Lyon

First printing, June 2018.

SCHOLASTIC

Once upon a time,
a queen wanted a pet.
"Bring me the best cat
in the land," she said.

People brought her lots of cats.
There were big cats
and small cats.

There were spotted cats
and striped cats.
But none of them was right.

One day, a man came to see the queen.
"I am Fred Fake," he said.
"This is the best cat in the land.
But only wise people can see her."

The queen did NOT see the cat.
But she wanted to seem wise.
So she lied, "Your cat is the best!"

"I must have it!" she said.
So she gave the man
a big bag of gold.

No one could see the Queen's cat.
But they wanted to seem wise.
So they lied, "Your cat is the best!"

One day, the queen decided
to have a cat parade.
She wanted to show off
her new pet.

People had big cats and small cats and spotted cats and striped cats. "Your pets are nice," said the queen. "But my cat is the best!"

People could NOT see the queen's cat.
But they wanted to seem wise.
So they lied, "Your cat is the best!"

A boy saw the queen march by.
The boy always told the truth.
"The queen has NO cat!" he shouted.

The queen heard the boy.
Oh my, he was right!
She didn't have a cat.

The queen stopped.
"You are a wise boy," she said.
"Thank you for being honest."

Then the queen saw a hungry cat
that had no home.
She picked it up.
"Come with me," she said.

"You are the best cat
in the land," she said.
Then they both lived
happily ever after.